I Want a Cuddle!

For Neil and for Lizzie who gave me the idea
MB

For my family
JP

ORCHARD BOOKS
96 Leonard Street
London EC2A 4XD
Orchard Books Australia
Unit 31/56 O'Riordan Street, Alexandria, NSW 2015
ISBN 1 84121 823 5 (hardback)
ISBN 1 84121 092 7 (paperback)
First published in Great Britain in 2001
First paperback publication in 2002
Text © Malorie Blackman 2001
Illustrations © Joanne Partis 2001
The rights of Malorie Blackman to be identified as the author and
Joanne Partis to be identified as the illustrator
of this work have been asserted by them in accordance
with the Copyright, Designs and Patents Act, 1988.
A CIP catalogue record for this book is available from the British Library.
1 3 5 7 9 10 8 6 4 2 (hardback)
1 3 5 7 9 10 8 6 4 2 (paperback)
Printed in Hong Kong/China

I Want a Cuddle!

Malorie Blackman

Illustrated by Joanne Partis

ORCHARD BOOKS

Little Rabbit and her friends
were playing peek-a-boo, when. . .

BUMP! THUMP!
Poor Little Rabbit!

"What's the matter, Little Rabbit?"
asked Hedgehog.
"I've hurt my paw and I want a
cuddle," sobbed Little Rabbit.
"I'll cuddle you," said Hedgehog.

"Ooh," said Little Rabbit. "You're too prickly." So off she hopped. . .

"Why are you crying, Little Rabbit?" asked Squirrel.
"I've hurt my paw and I want a cuddle,"
sniffed Little Rabbit.

"I'll cuddle you," said Squirrel.
"Ooh," said Little Rabbit, "you're too tickly."
Hoppity hop hop. . .

"Why are you so sad, Little Rabbit?"
asked Badger.
"I've hurt my paw and I want
a cuddle," said Little Rabbit.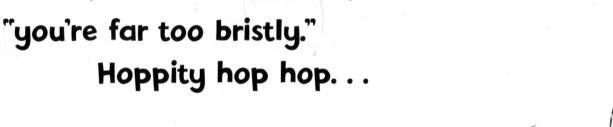
"I'll cuddle you," said Badger.
"Ooh," said Little Rabbit,
"you're far too bristly."
Hoppity hop hop. . .

"Hey! What's wrong, Little Rabbit?" asked Toad.
"I've hurt my paw and I want a cuddle,"
said Little Rabbit.
"I'll cuddle you," said Toad.

"Ooh," said Little Rabbit, "you're far too lumpy. And the bits that aren't lumpy are squidgy and bumpy! I want my mum."

And Little Rabbit set off home through the forest.

Little Rabbit was so busy hopping along. . .

that she didn't see who
was creeping and
sneaking up behind her. . .

Little Fox!

"What are you doing, Little Rabbit?" asked
Little Fox, licking his lips.

"I fell over and hurt my paw," said Little
Rabbit, "and now I'm going home for a cuddle."

And off Little Rabbit hopped. . .

"I'll **CUDDLE** you," said Little Fox.

OOOMPHS!

"No, thank you," replied Little Rabbit.

Hop! Jump!

"I'll **HUG** you then!" said Little Fox.

AAGH!

"No, thanks," called out Little Rabbit.

Hop! Jump! Skip!

"I'll give you a **BIG SQUEEZE** then!"

EEEEEEE EEK!

"I don't think so," said
Little Rabbit.
Hop! Jump! Skip! Leap!

"I'll **EAT YOU** then!" And Little Fox pounced at Little Rabbit.

But he missed.

Little Fox sat down,
opened his mouth and
HOWLED! "I want a cuddle.
I want a **CUDDLE.**"

Little Rabbit stopped.
Poor Little Fox!
Little Rabbit went over to
him, opened her paws and. . .

gave Little Fox a great
big cuddle!

"I'm going home to my Mum,"
sniffed Little Fox.

"So am I," said Little Rabbit.

"Thanks for the cuddle,"
said Little Fox.

"You're welcome,"
said Little Rabbit.

And hop! hop! went Little
Rabbit all the way home.

"Mum, Mum, I hurt my paw and Little Fox chased after me. I want a cuddle! Where's my cuddle?"

"Right here," said Mother Rabbit. And she cuddled Little Rabbit tight, tight, tight.

"Oh, Mum!" said Little Rabbit. "Your cuddle feels just right!"